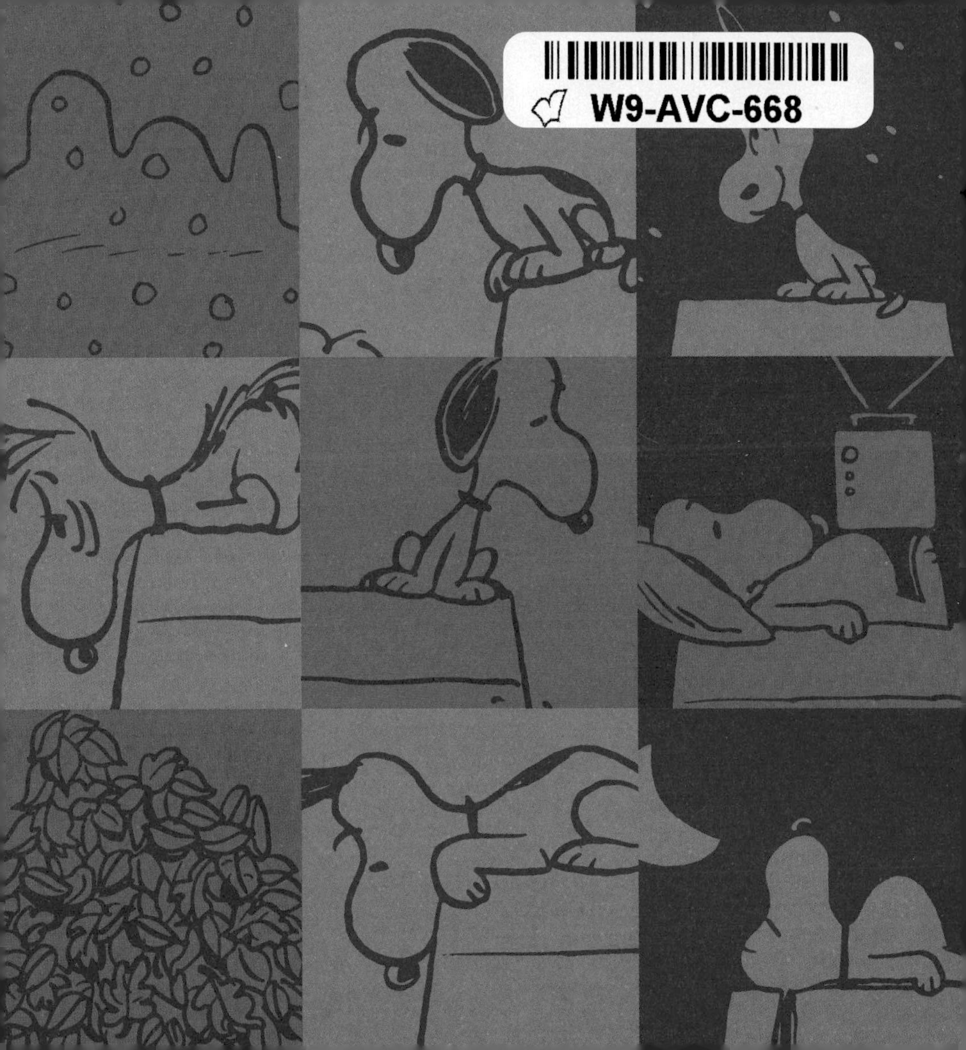

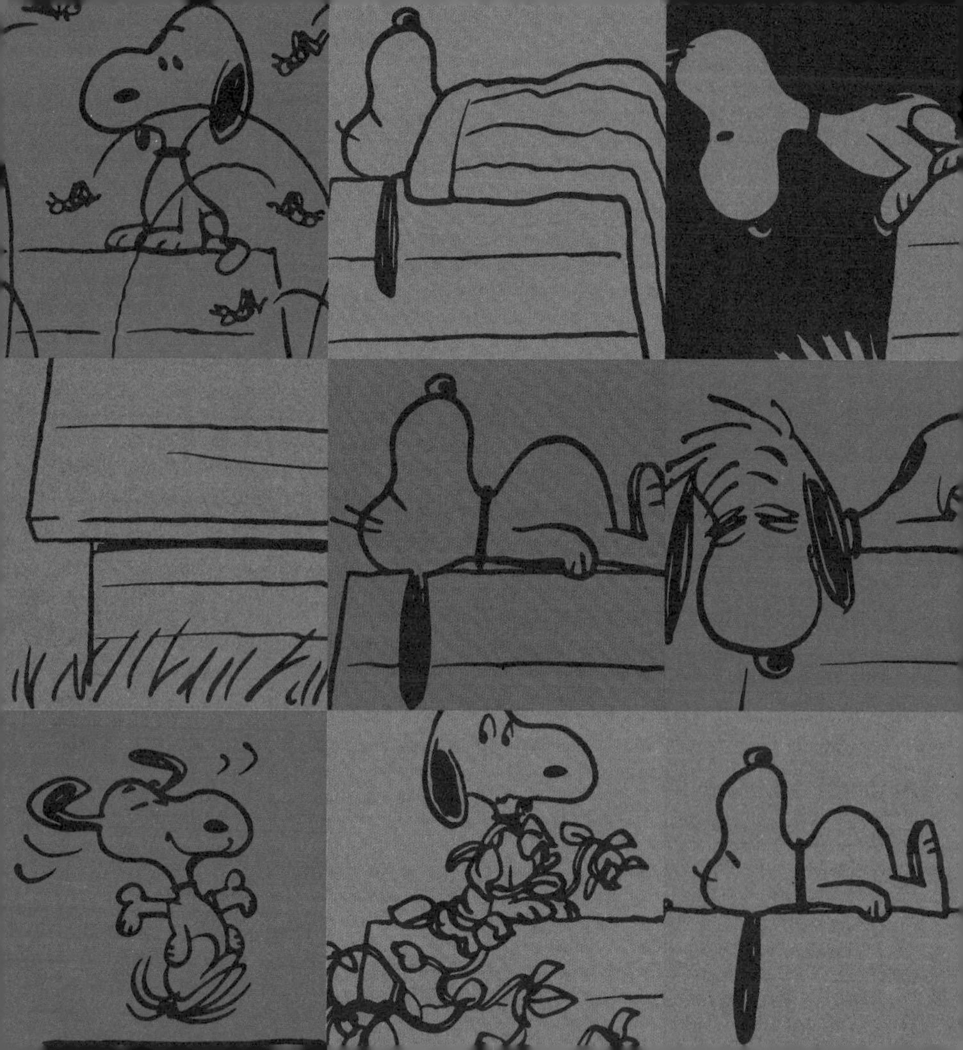

Home is
On Top of a
Dog House

ISBN-13: 9781604335781
ISBN-10: 1604335785
This book may be ordered by mail from the publisher.
Please include $4.50 for postage and handling.
But please support your local bookseller first!
Books published by Cider mill Press Book Publishers are available at special
discounts for bulk purchases in the United States by corporations, institutions, and
other organizations. For more information, please contact the publisher.
Cider Mill Press Book Publishers
"Where good books are ready for press"
12 Spring St.
PO Box 454
Kennebunkport, Maine 04046
Visit us on the web!
www.cidermillpress.com
Design by Jon Chaiet
Printed in China
1 2 3 4 5 6 7 8 9 0
First Edition

Home is On Top of a Dog House

BY CHARLES M. SCHULZ

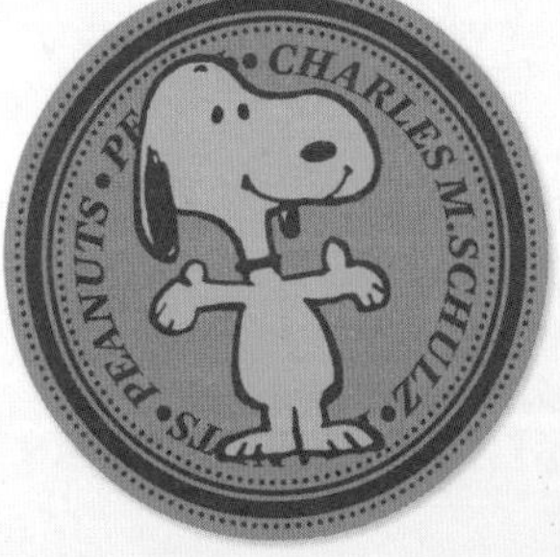
PEANUTS
CHARLES M. SCHULZ

Outer space fascinates me.

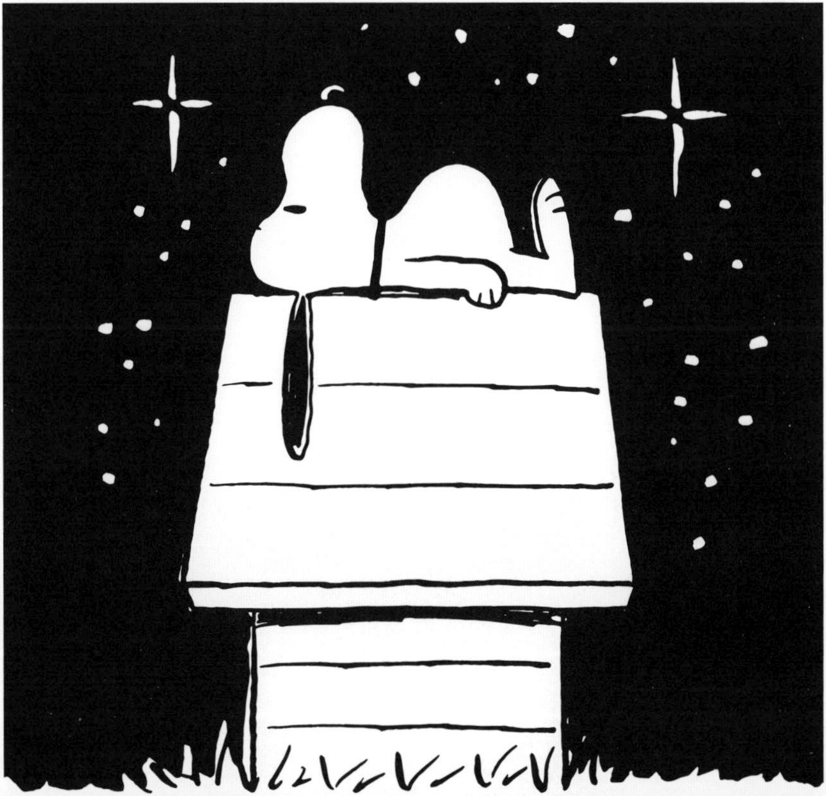

Show me a veterinarian, and I'll show you a man who loves to wield a needle!

I love to hear the patter of rain on the roof while I'm sleeping.

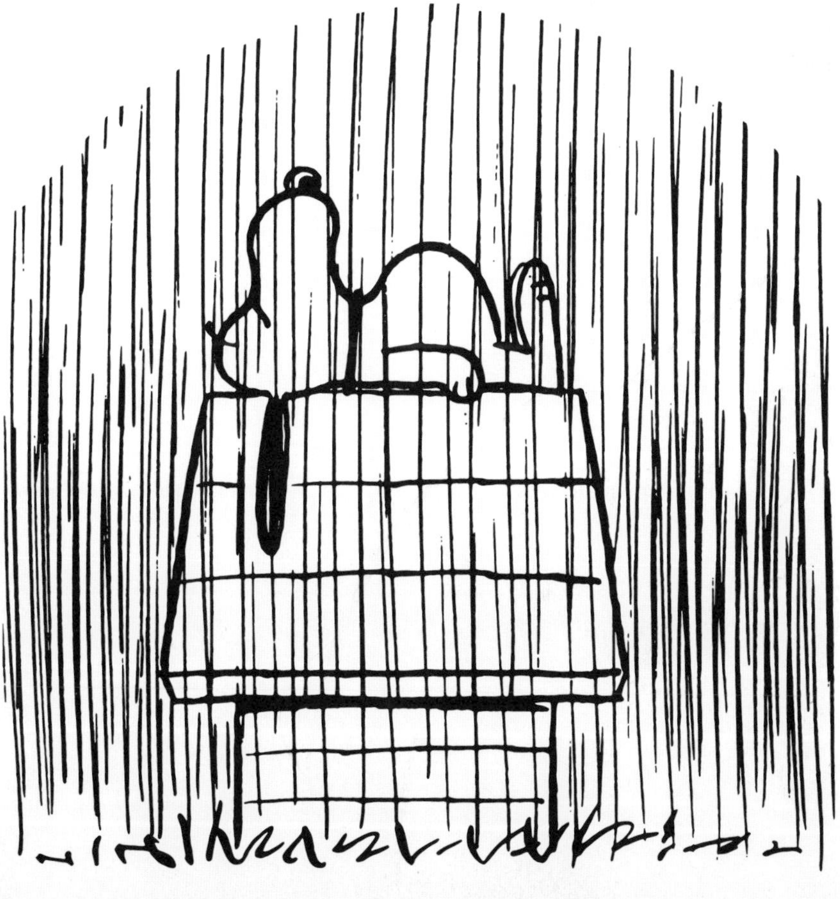

Snow is nice too.

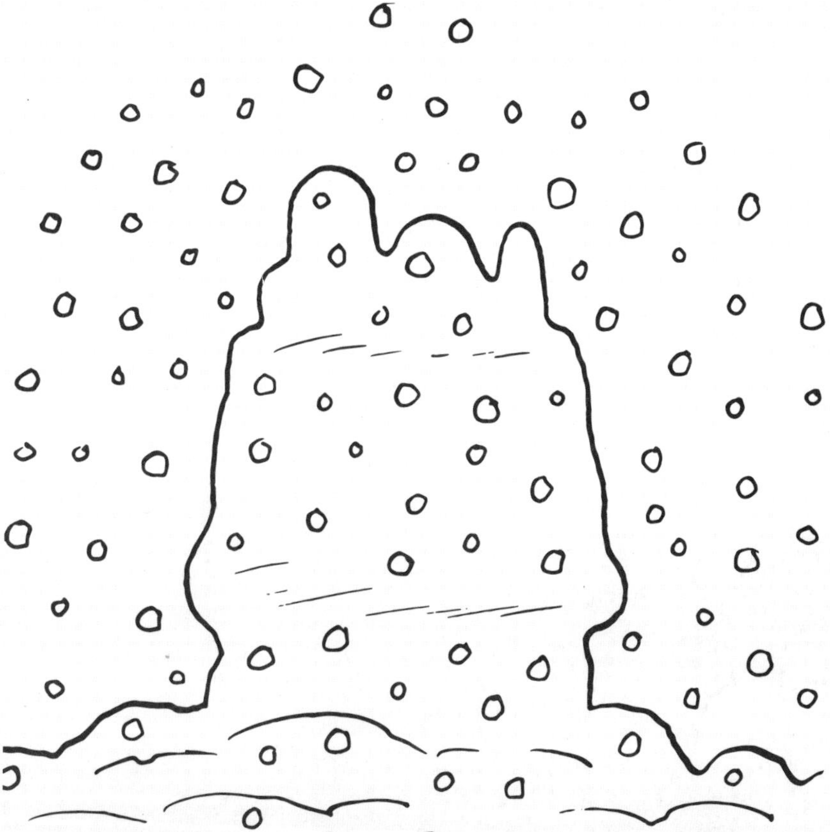

There's the ugliest sight in the world... an empty dog dish!

On a clear night I can get to Mexico City.

I miss Mr. Peepers.

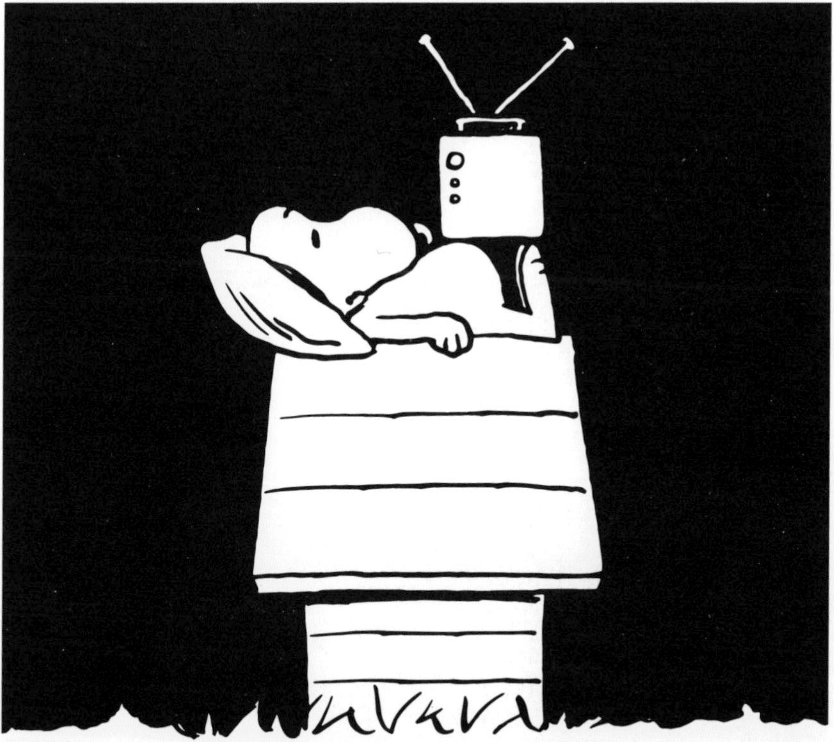

Some guys never really learn to do anything.

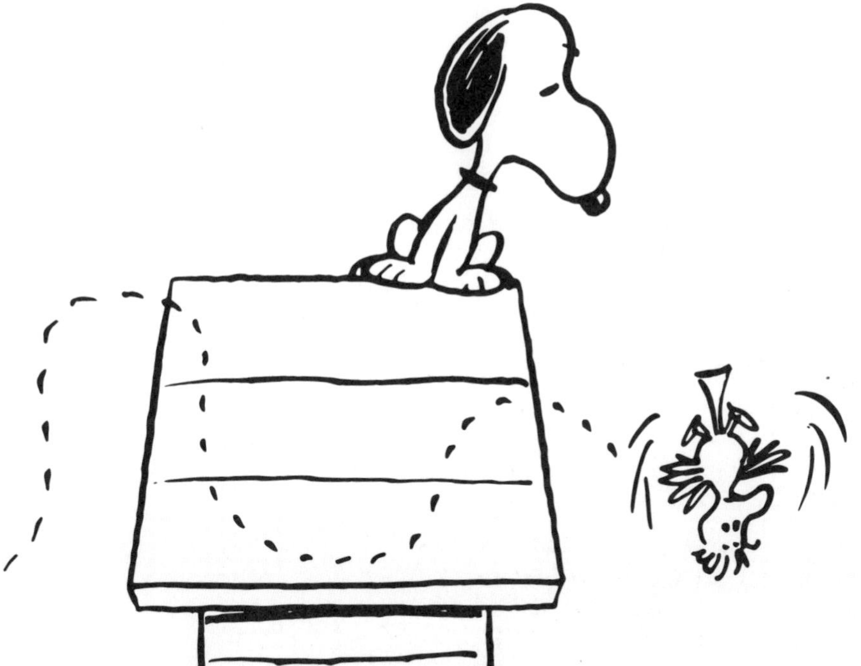

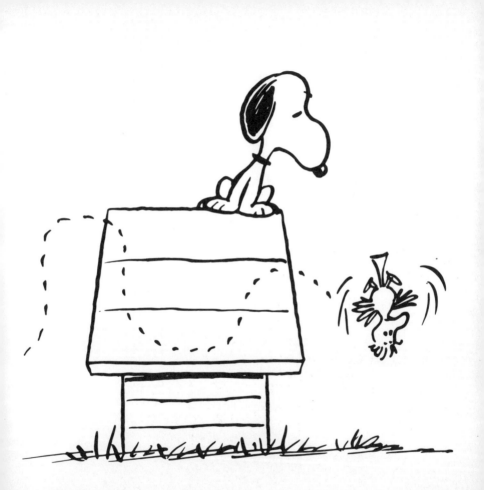

It is my humble opinion that a night's sleep dreaming of cats is no night's sleep at all.

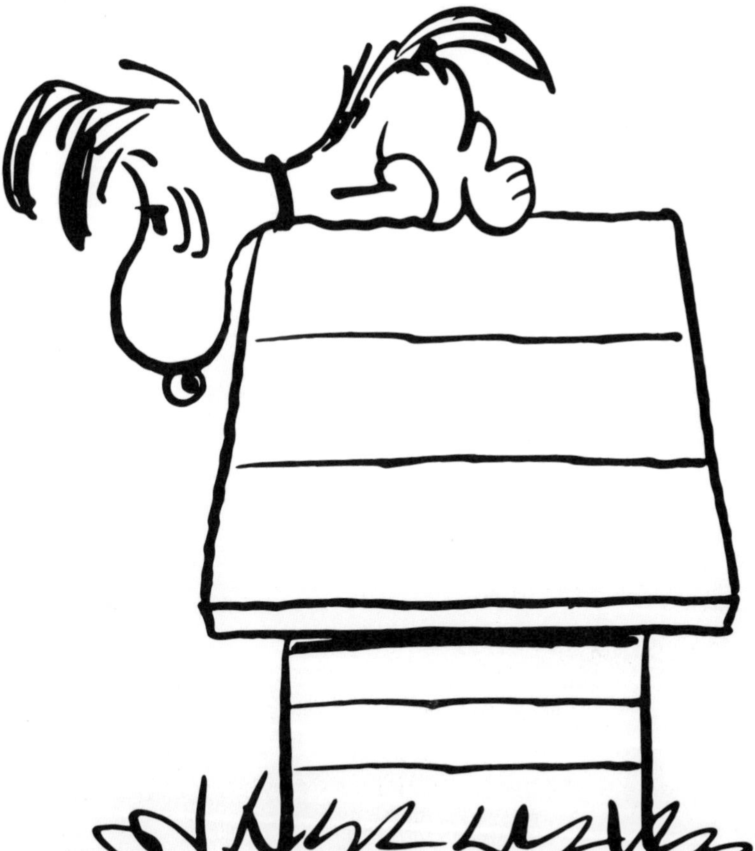

The only time I hear from the Daisy Hill Puppy Farm Alumni Association is when they want another donation!

How can you do
push-ups when your
nose gets in the way?

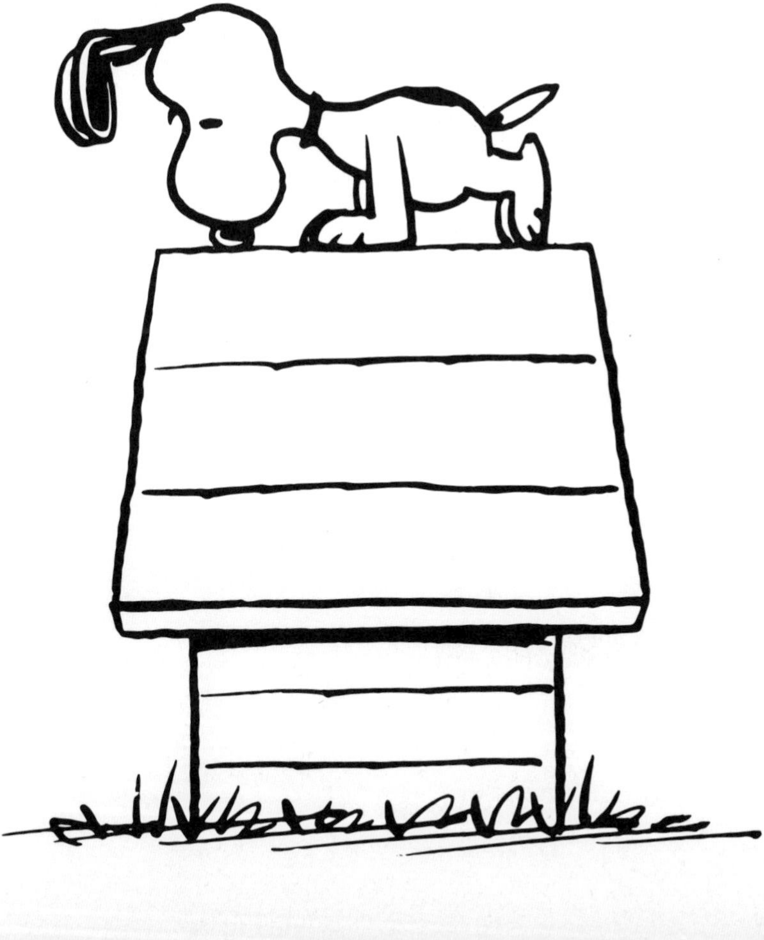

I always have a few friends over for Bridge on Thursdays.

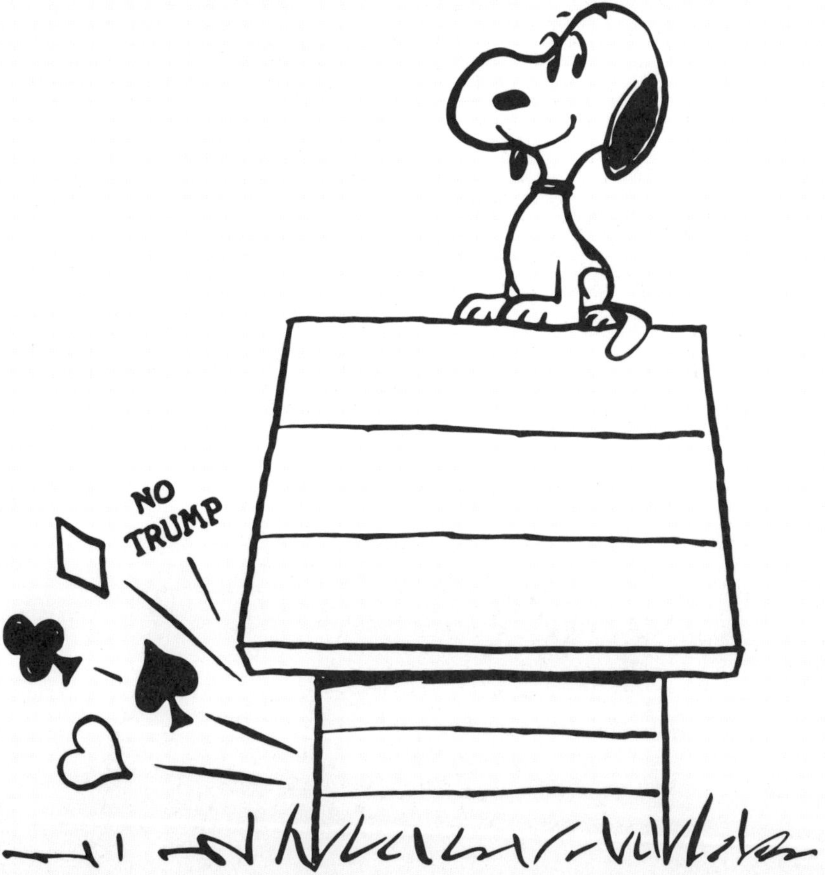
NO TRUMP

About five minutes of this is all I can take... then I get claustrophobia!

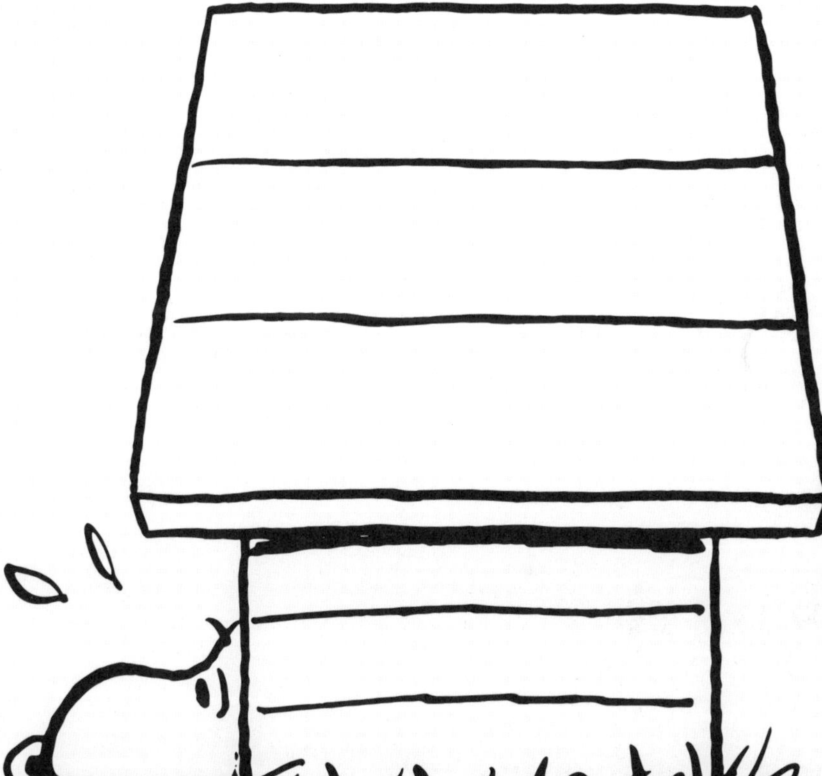

Commuter!

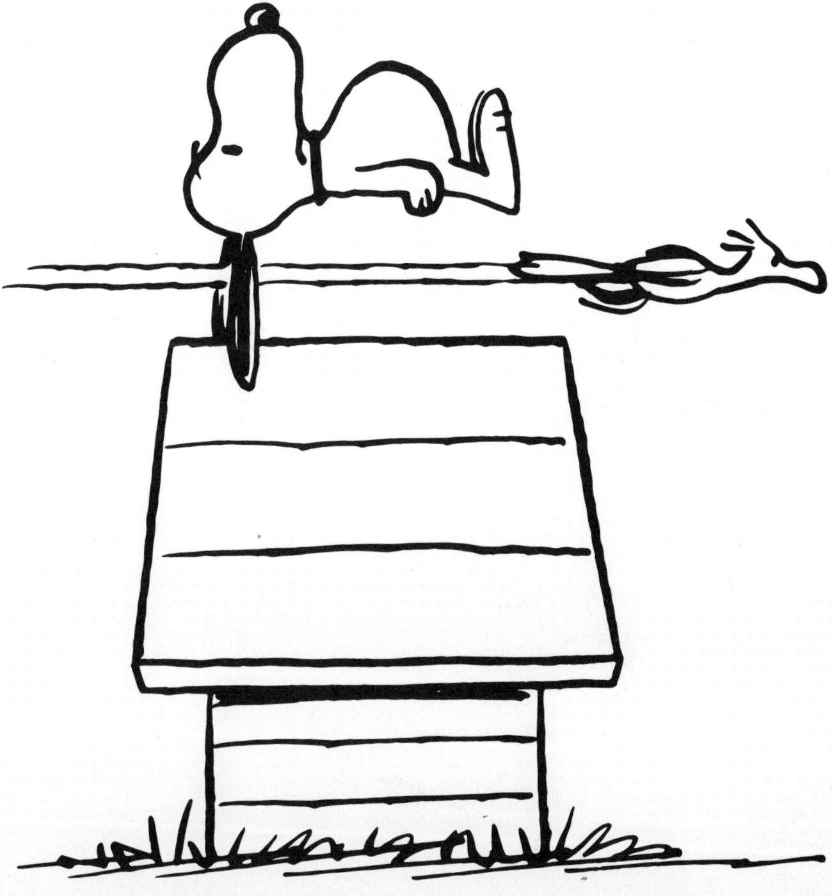

What do you do when
your National Geographics
begin to overflow?

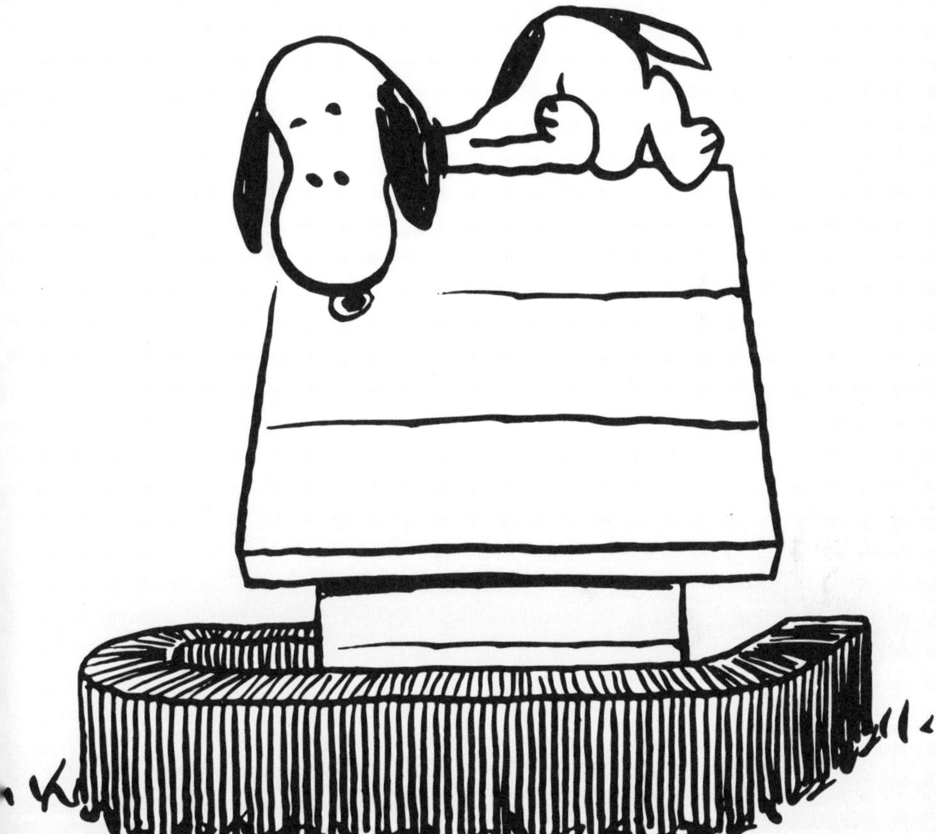

Is it fall already?

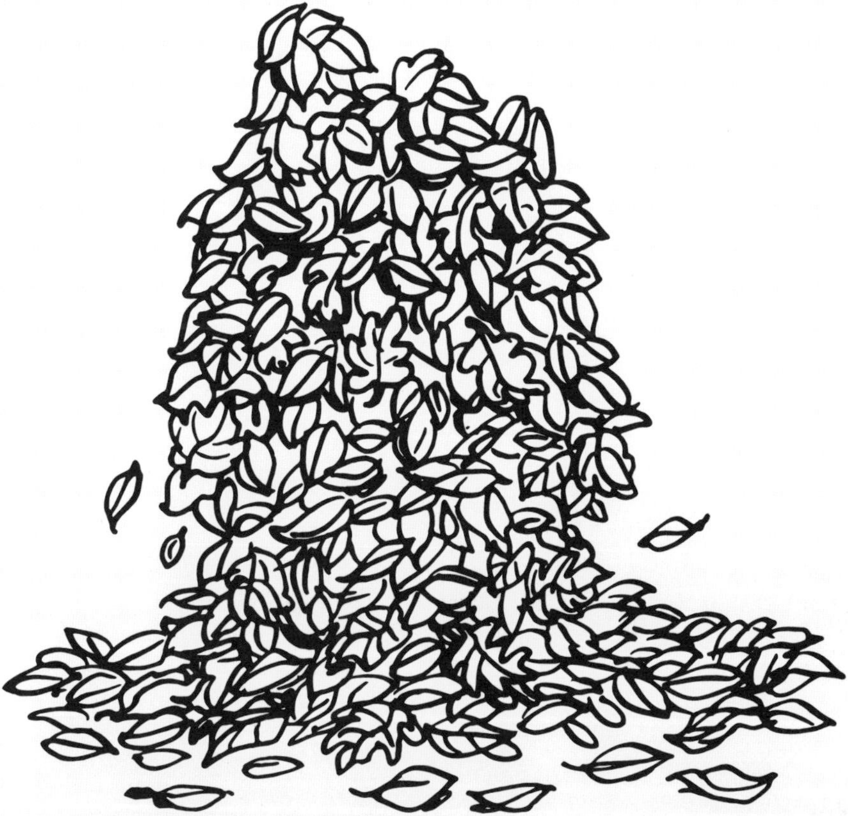

I live in constant fear that someone will break in and steal all of my Hank Williams records.

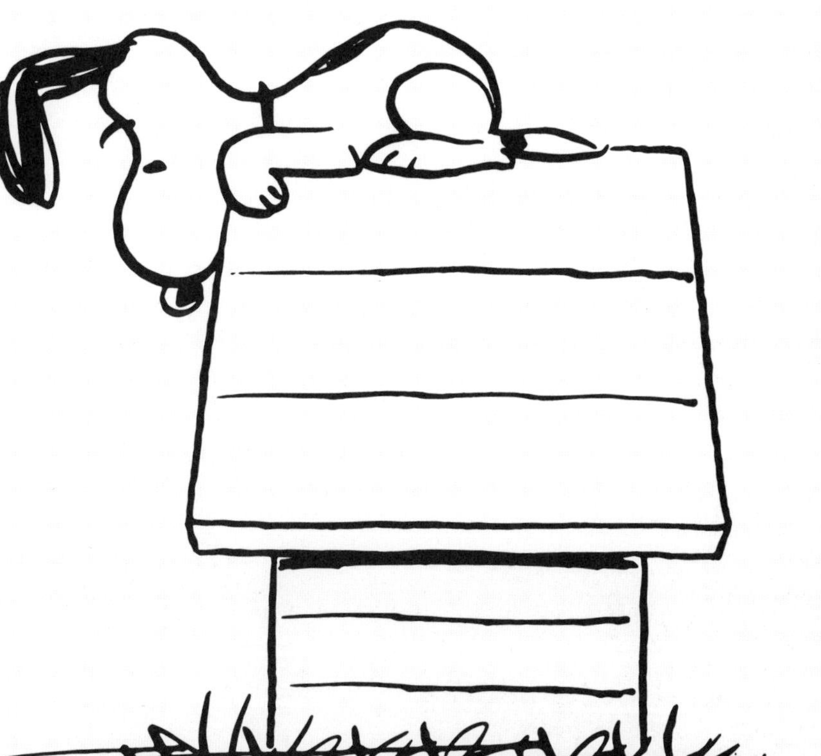

So what's wrong with having a night light?

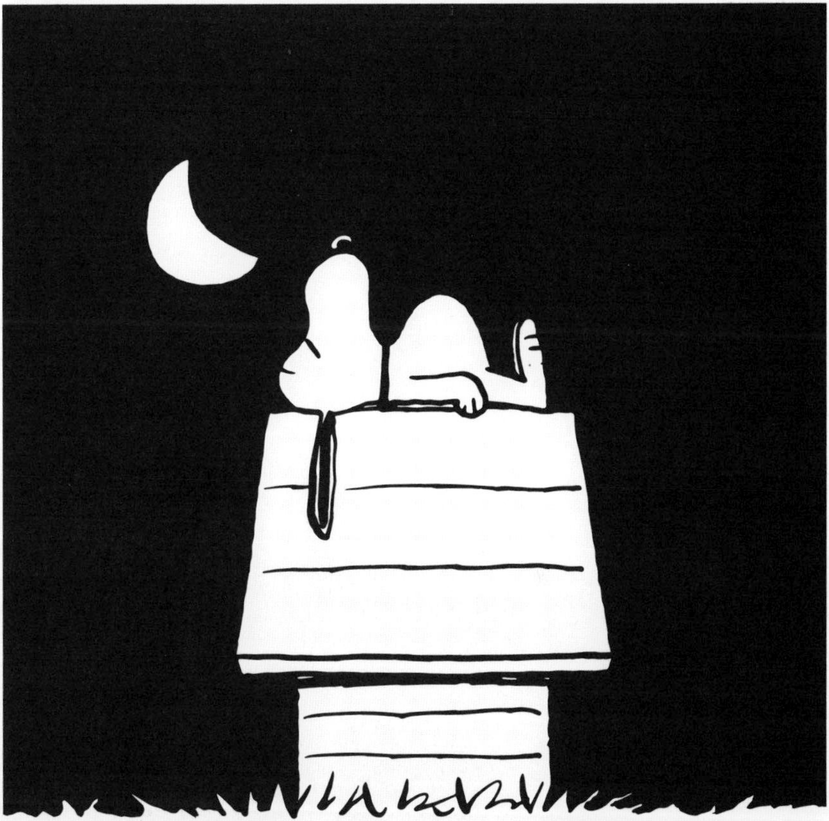

What terrible luck... I plan a picnic for today, and what happens? A locust plague!

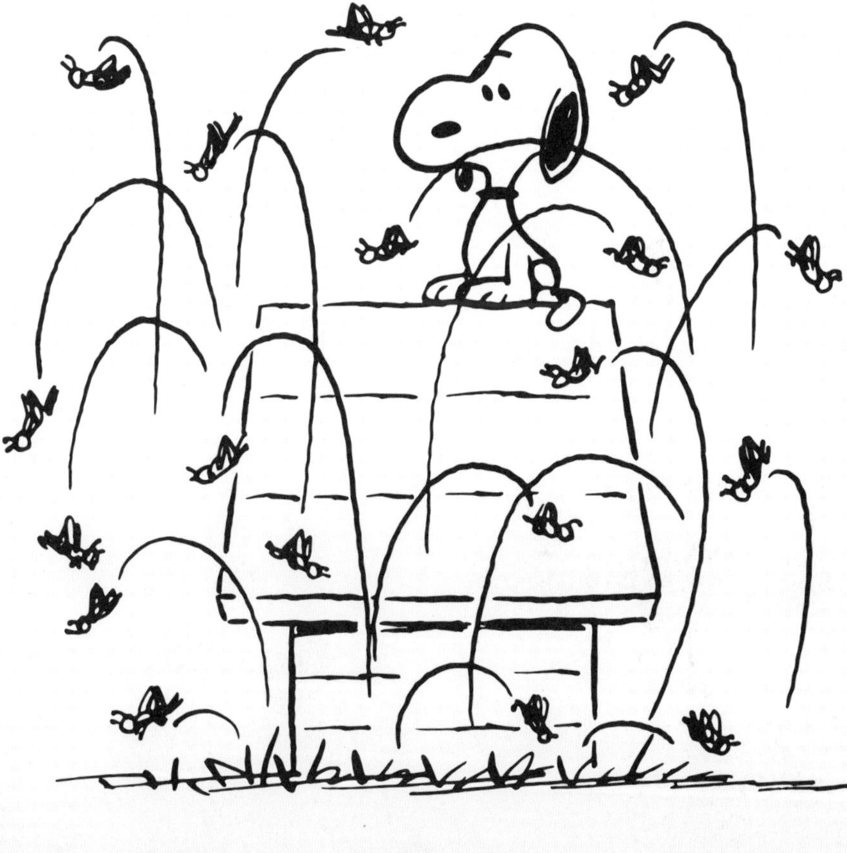

There's nothing like having a friend at the Army Surplus store.

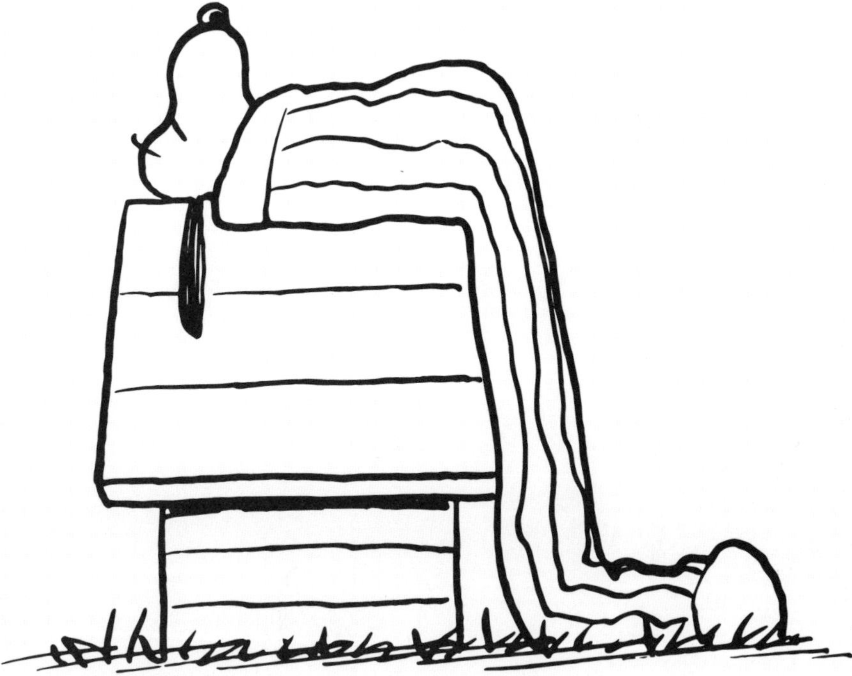

Rats! Someone left the light on over the pool table!

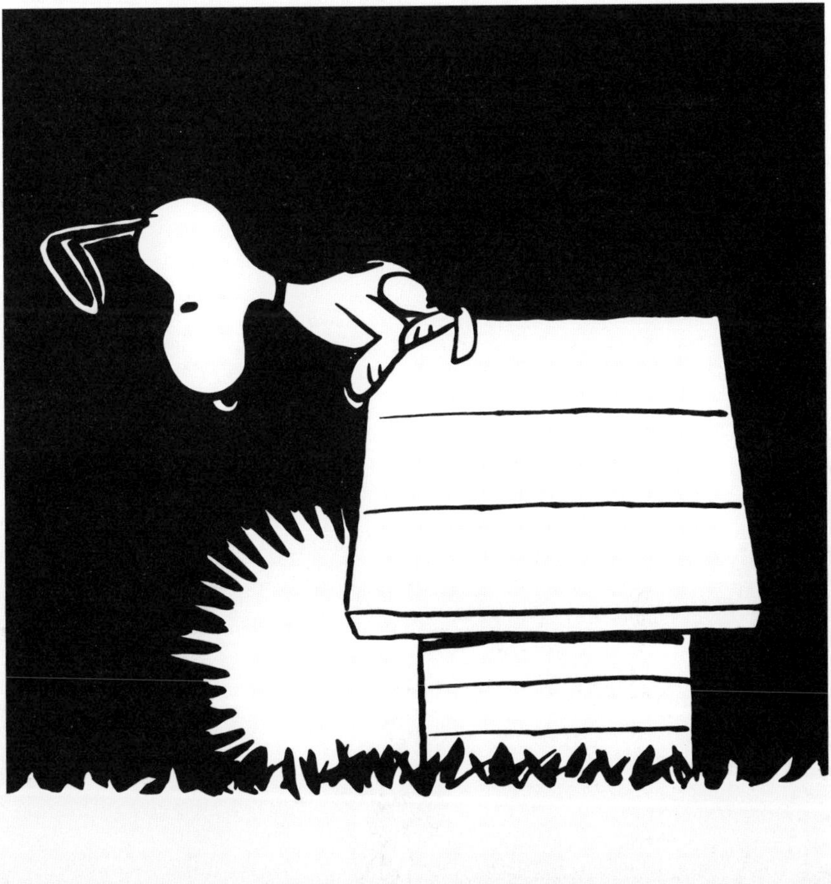

I think I'm allergic
to morning.

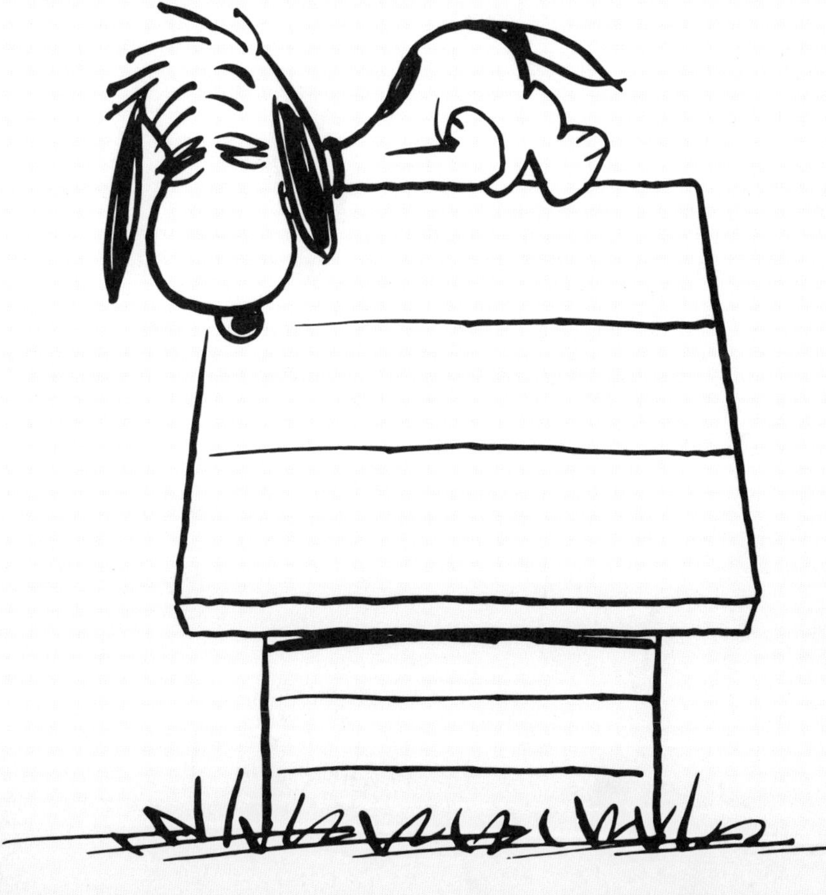

"Pigeons in the grass alas, Beagle on the roof aloof!"

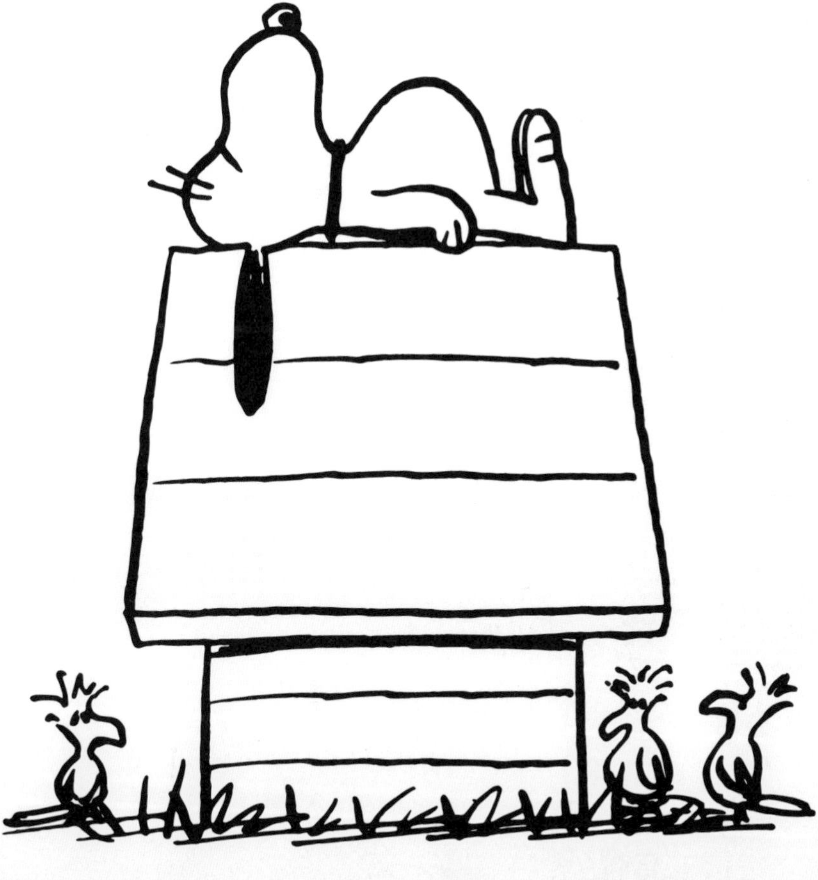

I hate windy days.

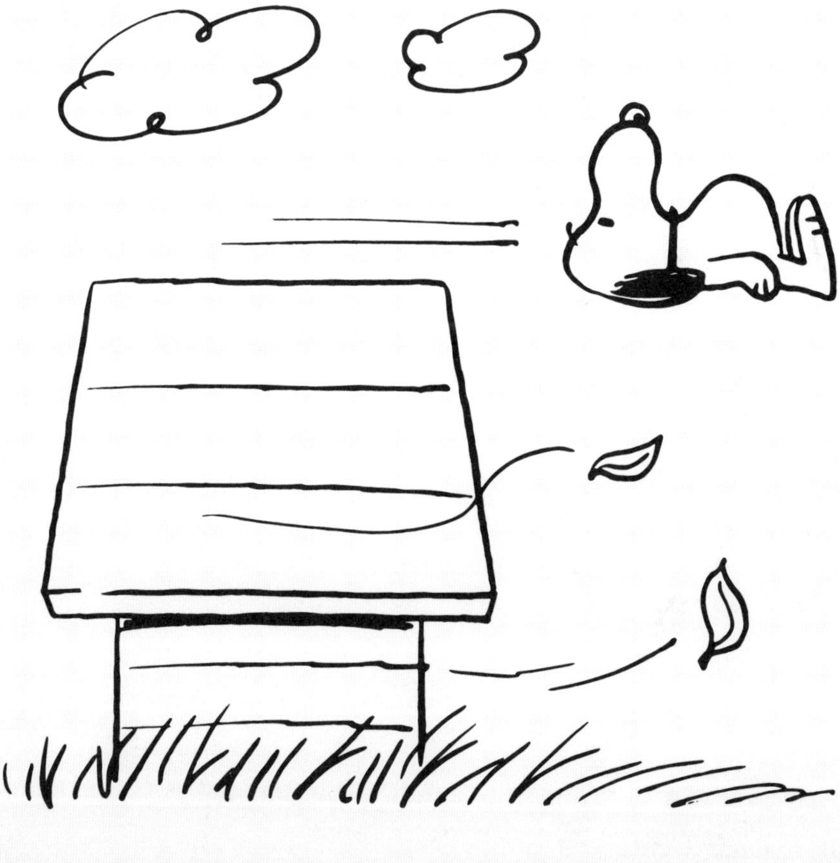

Who else do you know who can do the "Beagle"?

Actually, all I did was put this sweet potato in a jar of water, see... and... well...

Everyone should spend at least one night during the summer camping out.

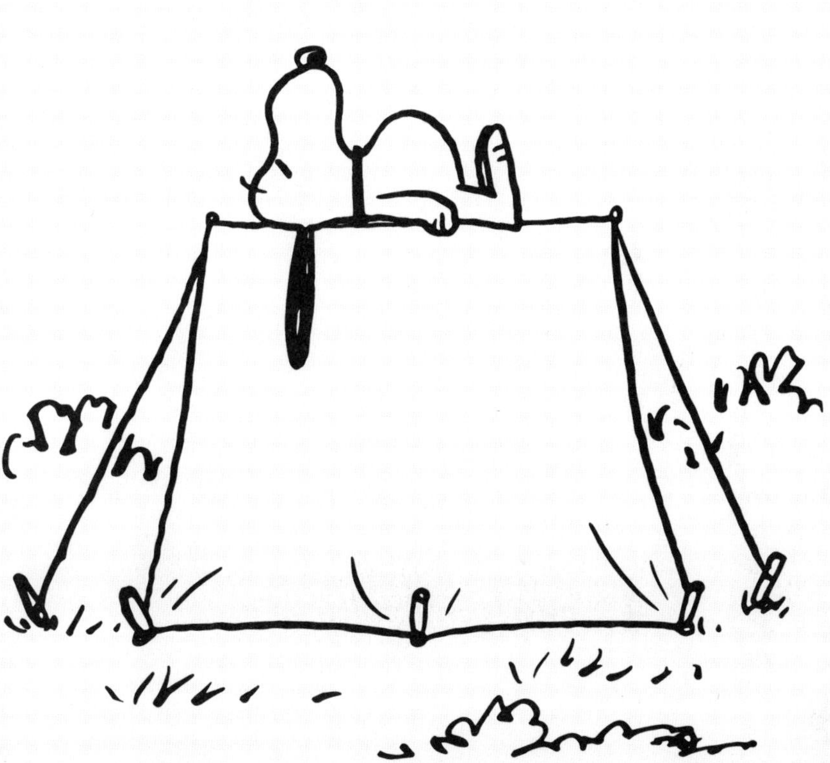

Have you ever had one of those days when you felt you just had to bite someone on the leg?

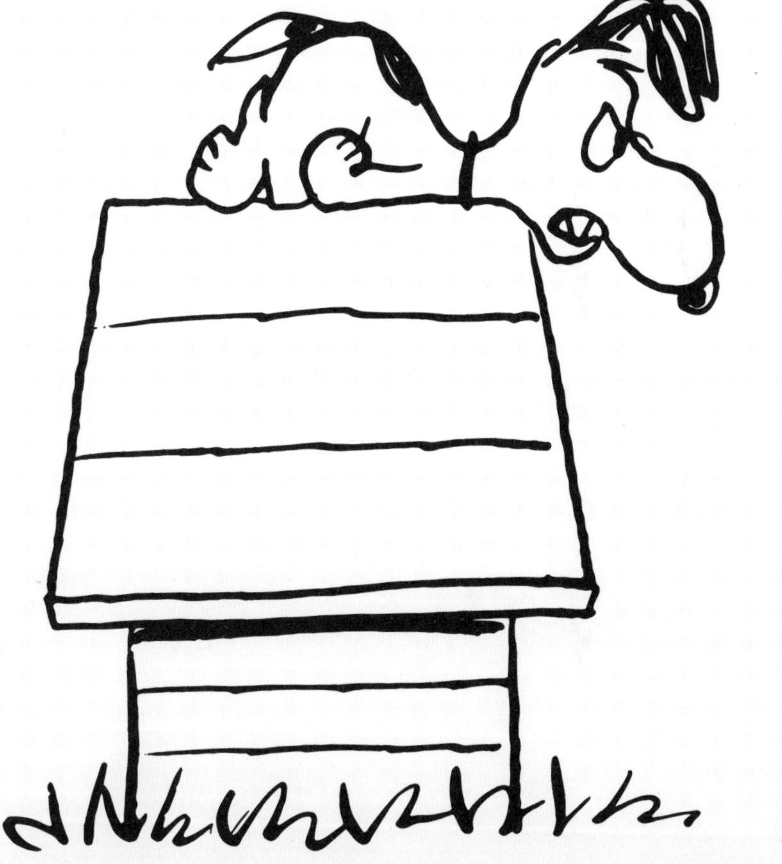

The worst part about living alone is not having someone to bring you tea and toast at bedtime.

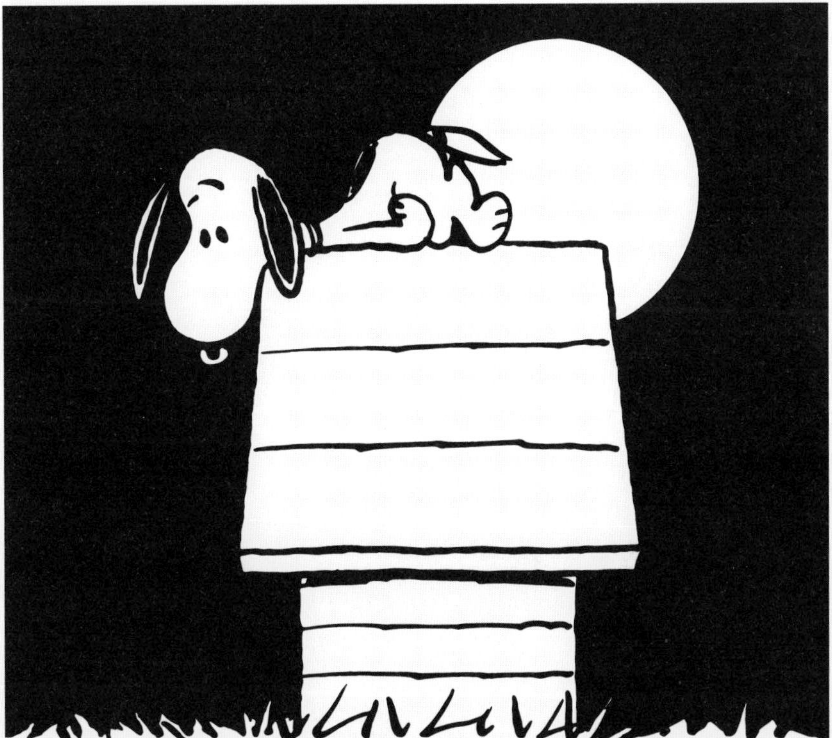

I do a lot of complaining,
but actually I love my home!

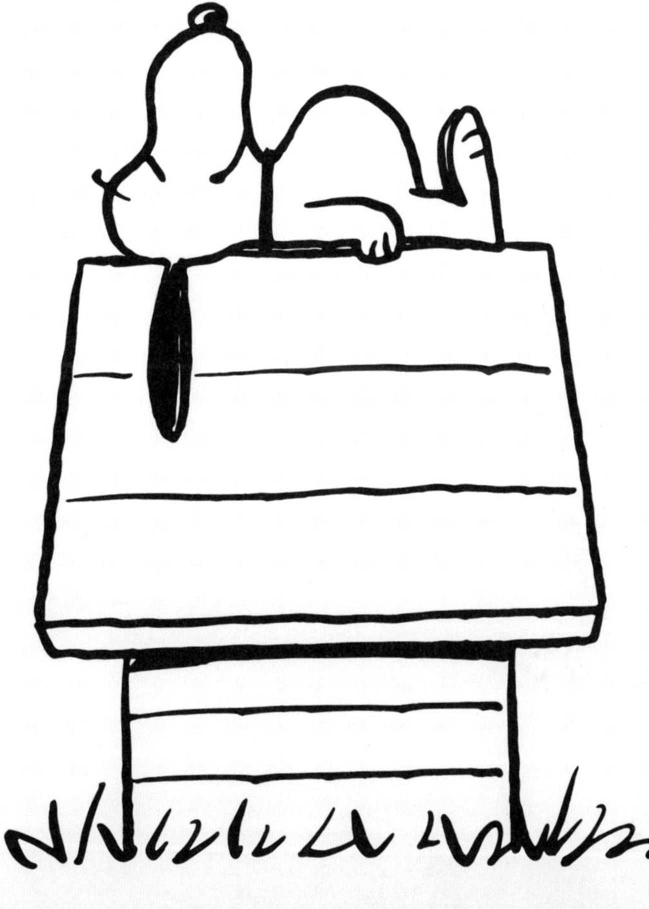

ABOUT CIDER MILL PRESS BOOK PUBLISHERS

Good ideas ripen with time. From seed to harvest, Cider Mill Press brings fine reading, information, and entertainment together between the covers of its creatively crafted books. Our Cider Mill bears fruit twice a year, publishing a new crop of titles each spring and fall.

VISIT US ON THE WEB AT
www.cidermillpress.com

OR WRITE TO US AT
12 Spring Street
PO Box 454
Kennebunkport, Maine 04046

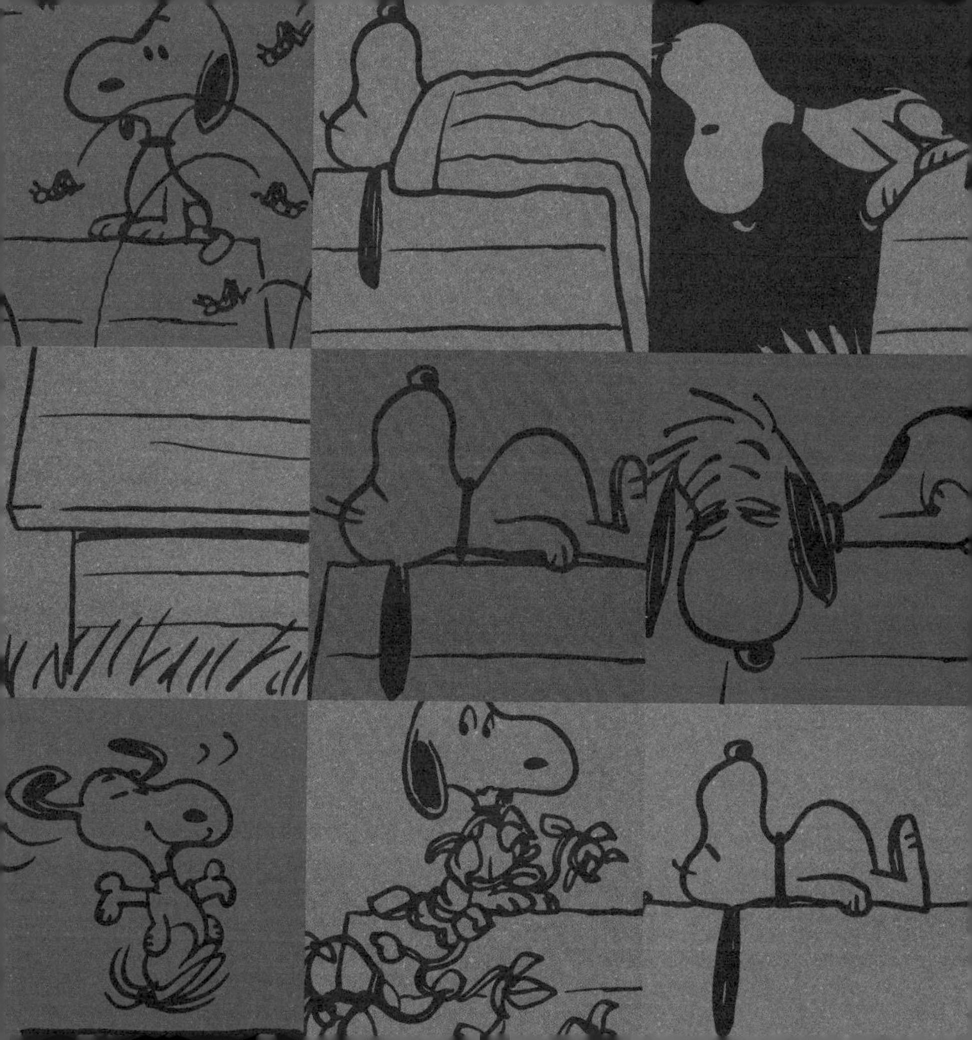

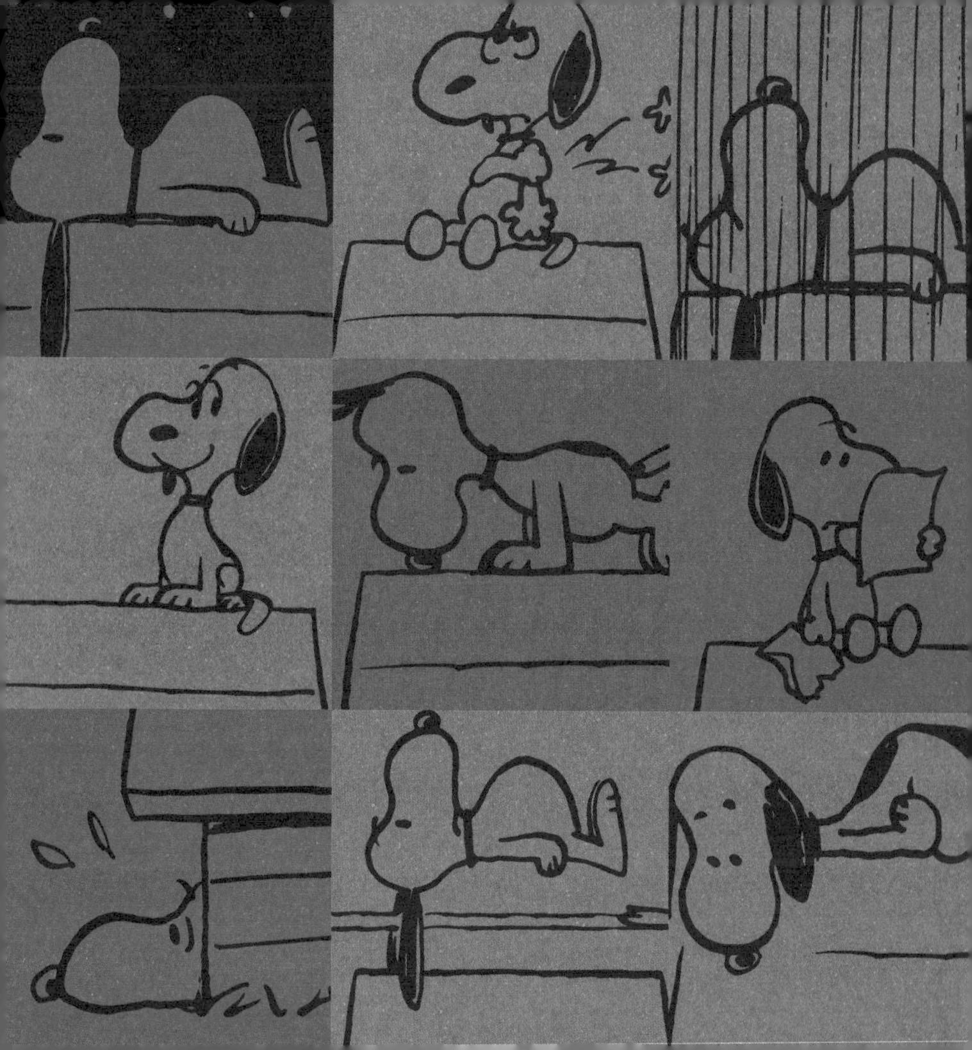